THE NOCTURNS

K.C. POTTORF

ILLUSTRATIONS BY CRAIG McKAY

For Luke and Haley
Who gave me a reason to write
stories like this one twenty years ago

CHAPTER ONE
THE BIG WOODS

IN THE NIGHT there is only darkness – darkness and the evil of which we do not speak. Allow me to explain. It's the same thing every evening in the Big Woods. The sun sets in the sky and the animals of the night known as the Nocturns make their way out of their hiding places and into the early moonlight. It's known as Twilight – the magical moment that is neither day nor night.

Thriving in the darkness is a way of life for my kind. Working, playing and planning for the upcoming seasons in the magic of the night is loved by all the Nocturns – all but one. Me.

My name is Howard. I'm *not* a Nocturn – at least not by choice. I'm Howard the Coward, and I'm a raccoon. Yep, that's what they call me. And get this – it was my dad's name too. There were two of us – *were*.

My dad died when I was just a kit – that's raccoon-speak for a baby. He was a guardian of the Big Woods, a Keeper of the Night, a hero. He died defending the Big Woods against the evil of which we do not speak. I'd tell you about that but no one speaks of it.

He was big and strong. I'm a smaller than average raccoon with the nickname *coward*—you can figure it out from there. I'm nothing like my dad.

I live with my mom, grandfather and my little sister in an oak stump on the edge of the Big Woods. We're a typical Nocturn family except for me. Which brings me back to my original point – it's Twilight…again and it's time for everyone to wake up and go to work or come out and play. But I've already been out all day. I don't like the night. I don't like the dark.

"Howard?" My mother called to me from inside the stump we called home. She was sweet and nice. She told me constantly how much she loved me. She also asked a lot of questions – a *lot* of questions. *Where have you been? Where are you going? Did you eat enough? Do you feel okay?* Yeah, a lot of questions.

"Yes?" I called into the stump.

"Come and eat breakfast."

"It's not breakfast to me," I uttered under my breath. I looked to the sky and saw the sun turning from orange to purple and dropped my shoulders in dread. The darkness wouldn't be far behind.

The evening breeze blew across my masked face and I nervously wrung my paws and paced around the top of the stump before going inside, thinking of ways to avoid going out for the night.

Don't get me wrong. I'm not *afraid* of the dark—I just want to truly understand the world I live in. Why is the sky clear some days and cloudy others? Why does the wind smell funny when the leaves begin to fall or just before it snows? I can't figure any of this out in the dark where I can't see anything. I need to be a daytime animal where I can see things as they really are.

Still, every night it happened. The sky turned orange and then purple and then it was dark. No light, no sun, only black. And still every night my family wondered why I didn't want to go out into the darkness.

"Howard!" I heard Grandfather shout. If I didn't get down there soon, having someone call me Howard the Coward was going to be the least of my worries. I hurried inside the old stump and found them all waiting.

"Sleeping in these days, huh?" Gran asked.

I started to tell him I'd been out all day, but thought better of it as my mom placed two steaming buckwheat cakes in front of me. "It's only six," I replied without looking him in the face.

"I've been up since four-thirty and I've already done a day's worth of work around here." My granddad always worked harder than everyone else and he wanted to make sure we all knew it. Lots of smart-mouthed comments filled my head, but if I wanted to slink back into the stump later and read instead of going out with everyone else, giving Gran lip wasn't going to help in that department. I knew the best way to handle it.

"I'm not as tough as you are, Gran." I gave him a nod and hoped the conversation would stop before it began.

"No one is," my mom said as she poured the maple syrup she'd gathered from a nearby tree on my cakes. I dove in headfirst, taking a huge bite.

"What are you up to tonight?" he asked.

I wiped the sticky sweetness from my mouth and wondered if it was a loaded question. "I don't know. What are you guys doing tonight?"

"Your mother and Violet are gathering berries for our winter food supply and I'm

going with them – in case they need help."
Gran looked away and gave my little sister
a pat on the head.

"We'll be fine, Dad, if you'd like to do
something else." I watched Mom sigh and
I knew she was perfectly capable of taking
care of herself and my little sister, but I
still liked the idea that Gran wanted to
protect her, especially since my dad wasn't
around.

"No, no. You never know what kind
of vermin you might meet gathering
berries. You might need me," he said with
a smile.

Mom paused and looked to me.
"Come with us?"

"Is that an invitation or an order?" I
asked.

"Well…." She hung on the word and
my nose began to twitch with anxiety.

"I'll be fine here by myself," I said
quickly, not wanting her to think her plans
over too long or begin to ask questions.
"Other raccoons my age are looking after
kits. If they can be trusted to take care of a

live kit, surely you can trust me to stay here by myself."

I watched the wheels turn in her head.

"You don't need to be staying in to-night, Howard. What are you afraid of?" she asked.

I slammed my paws on the table and stood in a huff. "For the last time, it's not logical to be out at night when you can't see anything. It's not that I'm afraid—daylight is where the action is. If I can't see, smell, taste, or hear it – it's not worth exploring."

They all gave me a blank stare. I was so angry I thought my head might explode as it pounded in sync with my beating heart.

My argument, no matter how well planned or executed, never worked. My family was dedicated to living life in the dark. I wanted to walk in the light. I wanted to discover and draw my own conclusions about life, not follow in the footsteps of everyone else. In fact I didn't want to follow in anyone's footsteps and they were all following one Nocturn – Nicodemus.

I lived with a group that didn't think for themselves. They were followers, not leaders and they only listened to Nicodemus – the commander of the Keepers of the Night.

I understood the logic in following a leader, but this guy was a piece of work. Nicodemus told of the coming seasons, how to prepare for the elements of nature the Nocturns would have to endure, and warned of the evil of which we do not speak. The Nocturns turned to Nicodemus for wisdom and guidance, and yet no one had ever seen him. He only spoke through his trusted messenger and fellow Keeper of the Night, Waldron. As far as I knew, Waldron was the only one who'd ever seen Nicodemus. This fact alone was reason enough for me to doubt the ways of the Nocturns. How could everyone take advice from a Nocturn they'd never seen or met?

Sure, Nicodemus had been right as far back as anyone could remember, but did that mean that *everything* he said was the only way?

Mom finally broke the silence with a sigh. "I want you to go out for a little while, Howard. I know your buddies Petey and Bo will be by at sunset," she said, referring to my two best friends. "I'm not taking no for an answer."

"Fine." I leaned against the wall and crossed my arms in protest.

"Howard, if your dad were alive he would want me to encourage you to get out," Mom said as she dropped her shoulders in disappointment.

"I'm *not* Dad and I never will be!" I shouted as I stormed off.

I needed to get away. I climbed up and out of the stump to sulk. "Why?" I shouted to the sky. "Why would I be placed here in the Big Woods only to suffer with a life that isn't right for me? It just isn't fair."

My shouting brought Violet outside. She emerged ready to play in the moonlight. "Whatcha doin', Howard?" Violet loved the night and she loved to talk about it. All. The. Time.

"Just hangin' out."

"Why don't you want the sun to go to bed? Don't you want to come out and play?"

"No," I snapped. "When have I ever been waiting for the sun to set? Just because you like the dark doesn't mean that I like the dark. Just because everyone else likes the night doesn't mean I have to. Just leave me alone, okay?"

I hopped off the stump and began to pace around a nearby tree and through the safety of Mom's flowers. I knew all of the flowers in the garden and it relaxed me to walk through them and recite each of their origins and what they could be used for. After calming down, I looked back at Violet and felt like a heel. She didn't deserve my attitude. After all, I *did* have a good life. I had a family who loved me, a grandfather who wanted to teach me everything just like he taught my dad and an overprotective mother.

My granddad was a hard working raccoon. His real name was Charlie but everyone called him Chevy. Why couldn't I have been named Chevy? That's a cool name. I knew there was a story about how he got the nickname but he never told me, always saying it didn't matter. I suspected it had something to do with the evil of which we do not speak, but again, we don't speak of it.

I looked over the horizon and shook my head. Tonight for some reason I had a bigger pit in my stomach than usual, and as I paced the garden smelling the flowers I thought maybe I'd fake a stomachache. Then I could play in the garden and go back inside the stump.

Just when I started to rub my furry belly and put on my best *I think I'm going to be sick* face, I heard rustling behind me. "Why are you pacing, son?" Gran asked.

I nervously walked through the flowers, wringing my paws. "Just admiring Mom's flowers. She's very good at picking certain kinds that have healing properties." I continued to carefully skim the blooms ever so lightly with my paw, desperately trying to mask my fear. "And they smell nice too."

"That's because it's Twilight."

I went to grab my belly and fall to the ground when Violet popped into view. "Tell the story of Twilight again. Please?" she asked, rocking back and forth on her heels. "Is that when the flowers smell the very best?"

"Everything is better at Twilight, Violet. Twilight is one of the most precious moments of the day for a Nocturn."

Gran walked to our stump and looked behind to see if we were following. It was clear he wanted us both to pay attention.

"Every day just before the sun goes down and the moon comes out," he began as he reached his paw to the sky. "There is a perfect moment in time – Twilight. It's when everything stops, and for a moment you can be one with all that is perfect and good in the world. It's the earth's way of saying, *everything you did today is in the past and tomorrow you can start anew.*"

Gran lifted his paws to the sky and closed his eyes, allowing the setting sun to illuminate his furry face. He dropped his arms and gazed back at Violet who was giving him her undivided attention. "We are all here for a reason, Violet."

"What's the reason?" she asked as she looked up to him. Her tiny body was bathed in the setting sun and I knew she admired my grandfather. I did too, but that didn't make me a Nocturn.

"I know the reason," I mumbled under my breath. "To stay away from the evil of which we do not speak."

Gran gave me a stern look, shook his head and immediately turned his attention back to Violet. "It's different for everyone," he said.

"So how do you know?" Violet asked as I moved in closer too. I'd heard this speech hundreds of times and really didn't want to hear it again, but after the stink-eye he gave me I knew I should be more respectful.

"Because you do," he said kneeling down and giving Violet a warm and loving embrace. "It's the Nocturn way."

He patted her on the back and Violet hurried off to play, satisfied with his answer. He knew I wasn't so easily convinced.

He rose from the ground slowly. Years of work and the hard winters in the Big Woods had taken a toll on him. After a pause he turned to me. "And what are your plans again for this fine and beautiful evening?"

"Um…" I hesitated. "To wait for Petey and Bo."

"You've got to get out, son."

"I don't want to."

"Why? Because you're afraid of the dark?"

"I'm *not* afraid," I whined, pointing into the deep of the Big Woods. "Seriously, anyone who uses their head to think would say there is nothing out there but darkness."

"Howard, you're a raccoon and more importantly, you're a Nocturn."

"I don't want to be a raccoon! I'll be anything! Anything but me!"

Gran walked to me and we stood nose to nose. He put his paw on my shoulder and looked me directly in the eye, making me feel like he was about to dispense some life-changing wisdom. "We don't get to pick who we are in the world. You are nothing less than yourself, Howard. You will always be a raccoon, and you will always be a Nocturn. What you do with that is entirely up to you."

I looked at my feet, unable to speak.

"Waldron came to me today – just as he came to me years ago when your dad was young. Howard, Waldron wants to speak with you about the Keepers of the Night."

"What? Why?"

"Because like your father, you're a chosen Nocturn."

"I don't want to be *chosen*," I cried. "I'm not Dad. I'm Howard the Coward. Remember?"

"The evil of which we do not speak is out there, son. We need every Nocturn on alert, especially the bright ones and there's no one smarter than you. That's why he wants you."

"Can I be a Keeper of the Night during the day?"

"You know, son, just because you're awake during the day doesn't mean you're not living in the dark. You are." He walked away and just when the night couldn't get any darker or worse – it did.

CHAPTER TWO
FOREVER FRIENDS

MY BEST FRIEND Bo arrived right on time. I could smell him before I could see him and it was rank.

"Dude!" I shouted. "Can you not?"

He laughed and took a bow, proud of his stench. "A belch is just a gust of wind that comes from the heart. But should it take a downward turn, it changes to a —"

"I get it!" I shouted as I held my hand up to block his rhyme *and* his smell.

"I had to let it rip," Bo confessed with a smile. "Better out than in, right?"

Bo was a striped skunk. Named for his grandfather, Old Beauregard, I liked to tease him that B.O. was short for body odor. Bo never thought it was too amusing. He was funny, athletic, and smooth with the girls – all the things I was not. When faced with an occasion he couldn't put into words, he would put together phrases that made absolutely no sense and usually had something to do with the weather. This only made him more appealing to all our other friends. He could always make them laugh.

"Monkey trumpets in a hail storm," he said. "I thought Petey was already here. I wanted to gas you both."

"Sorry to disappoint you." I shook my head and held my nose. "He's not here yet."

Bo and I had been best friends as far back as I could remember. Bo was the Nocturn that all the other young Nocturns wanted to be and he loved to tell jokes – bad jokes. When he talked about anything or told a story with any amount of enthusiasm, he always raised an eyebrow and got a twinkle in his eye. He invariably seemed fearless, even when I knew he was scared to death. I always secretly wished, aside from the occasional smell, that I could be more like him. Bo was the Nocturn I always thought my dad would've wanted as a son. Bo should be a Keeper of the Night. Not me. Not Howard the Coward.

"What up, bro?" He slapped my paw above our heads, giving me a high five.

"Not much."

"We hangin' out tonight?" he asked as he climbed up on the stump next to me and looked over all that was the Big Woods.

"Sure, when Petey gets here."

Petey was a possum. He was nearly the same size and age as Bo and I but had a funny way about him that sometimes made him seem younger. Jumbling up his words, at times Petey didn't make sense. Other times his strange behavior made him wise in ways I could never explain.

Petey had many talents. He could hang by his tail and he was always either eating something or looking for something to eat. Consequently he was great at garbage grabbing – something I would never do. The smelly garbage and the threat of getting caught outweighed the food, fun and the thrill of doing something we weren't supposed to be doing. However, when Petey would find books in the garbage he would always bring them to me because he knew I loved to read. He was always happy to add to my library.

Bo and I sat together and waited. If Petey took too much longer I'd never leave the stump. It would be too dark and I was only staying out until the stars started to shine.

"What do you get if you pour hot water down a rabbit hole?" Bo asked.

"I have no idea," I replied sarcastically. I knew he was just trying to fill the empty silence between us.

"Hot cross bunnies!" he shouted and began to laugh hysterically as he elbowed me in the ribs making my already nervous stomach jump. "Get it?"

"I get it."

"Get it?" he asked again as he jabbed me in the ribs and knocked me off the stump.

"Very funny," I said, shaking my head and picking myself up off the ground. I knew Bo was trying to cheer me up. It was the same routine every night—Bo and Petey begging me to come out and play and me agreeing to go until the stars began to shine.

Bo was still laughing hysterically at his own joke and telling a new one as Petey came over the hill.

"What do you get when you cross a duck with a firework?"

"What?" I asked reluctantly.

"A fire quacker!" Bo screamed with delight.

Ignoring his second bad joke, I waved to Petey on the horizon.

"What's so funny? And *what* is that smell?" Petey's voice cracked as he shoved a blackberry into his mouth.

"What do you think it is?" I rolled my eyes and pointed twice behind Bo's back. "Bo pushed me off the stump and now he thinks he's hilarious. You know what happens when he gets excited."

"I had to let it rip, man. I must say I'm kinda proud of that one."

"Dude." Petey screwed his face into a tight knot, letting Bo know his latest odiferous cloud of stench wasn't appreciated. "I'm eating here."

"You're always eating," Bo said in protest but then suddenly giving in. "Fine. I'm sorry."

We both knew he wasn't sorry at all and I nervously walked away listening to my two best friends razz each other. I kept looking to the sky, pacing and wringing my paws.

"So what's on the menu tonight, boys? We could mess up the trash really good. Kit the Cat always blamed gets for it," he said. jumbling up his words. "It's classic."

I stopped in my tracks, closed my eyes and clenched my fists, frustrated by Petey's tangled sentence. "You mean *gets blamed for it*," I said slowly to make my point.

"That's what I said," Petey quipped, completely unaware once again of what he'd said. "Or we could go and bug old man Evron."

"That old coot?" Bo asked. "He's blind as a…well, you know."

"Well, he *is* a bat," Petey added as if we didn't already know.

"Gran says he used to know the Big Woods better than anyone," I said.

"Yeah," Petey added. "He was a Keeper of the Night. The Messenger, like Waldron."

"Waldron," I muttered as I thought of my conversation with Gran. "The guy who gets *his* information from *another* guy. Doesn't anyone look around at what's going on and make some decisions instead of all this backwoods, in-the-dark thinking?"

"I myself for my think."

Bo and I exchanged smiles, knowing it wouldn't be the last time Petey would mix up his words tonight.

"I think his brains are scrambled," Bo said to me under his breath.

"I heard that," Petey snapped.

Bo smacked Petey on the back, causing him to sputter before he gave us *his* idea of the big plan for the night. "I say we head down to the other side of the Big River. I heard there were some cute young kits out and about from last spring," crooned Bo.

I knew he only wanted to see the girls. Why wouldn't he? They all loved him.

"Is that all you ever think about, Bo? Girls?" Petey asked. "Dude, you always want to go and check out the new stripes across the Big River. I'm vetoing that one tonight. It's all bros tonight. No girly kits."

As Petey and Bo bickered back and forth, I sat. I had no opinion. I watched the light diminish from the sky. I didn't want to go anywhere. The darker it got, the bigger the pit in my stomach became.

"Howard?"

"Huh?" I asked, dazed and still in my own world.

"What do *you* want to do tonight?" Petey asked.

Bo grabbed me by one arm. "Come on, let's go. We're doin' *something* – anything!"

Petey took me by the other shoulder and the three of us began to walk into the Big Woods arm in arm. I looked to the sky and noticed the orange had turned to purple and blue. I didn't know how long I could stay out in exact minutes, but I told myself I couldn't clearly see the stars just yet so I was safe for a little bit longer.

As the three of us meandered through the Big Woods, Bo and Petey laughed and joked and I continued to watch the sky. I wanted to be a part of the conversation, but I was finding it hard to concentrate on anything other than how I would get back and the impending darkness.

"I'm just saying, road kill would be an awesome costume for you, dude."

"Bo, I think you are taking the *playing possum* thing a little too far," replied Petey as he stopped to stuff another blackberry into his mouth from the vines growing on the fence post.

"That time you pretended to be dead for a week – remember? You were going for a record and I helped out and put a little stink on you. Howard made tiny splints to hold your legs in the air for days?" Bo said as he reenacted Petey lying on the ground with all four paws in the air. "*That* was one of the greatest things I've ever witnessed."

"What do *you* think, Howard?" Petey mumbled through a mouthful of berries.

"Nah, it's not too dark yet," I replied, not listening to their conversation. "I'll stay out a little bit longer."

"Dude!" shouted Bo, punching his finger into my chest. "I'm not letting you bail on us. Come on!"

With that Bo rolled his eyes and took off. When he realized he was running by himself he stopped and shouted back, "C'mon! Let's go! It won't hurt you to stay out for a little while."

"It'll be fine," Petey agreed as he stuffed another berry into his mouth, giving me a smile as the dark juice ran down his face.

"Come on, you slowpokes!" Bo shouted.

"Okay," I agreed with a nod.

Petey and I took off running through the Big Woods and I had to admit it felt awesome as the wind blew through my fur and all the smells of the Big Woods invaded my senses.

Bo waited at the top of the first hill for us. "You guys are such lollygaggers."

"What in the Sam Hill is a lollygagger?" Petey asked as we finally caught up.

"We're never gonna pick up cute furry things with big beautiful eyes that think we are the best thing that ever roamed the night if you say things like *Sam* and *Hill*." Bo put his hands on hips and leaned into Petey. "Sometimes I really question my judgment in hanging out with you."

"Bo, Petey," I hissed as I grabbed them both by the fur on their chest. "Could you both shush?" I put a finger to my lips and whispered, "Do you hear that?"

Bo walked away and put a paw to his ear and mocked me while Petey stood on his hind legs and lifted his pink nose to the air to sniff. I felt the already deep pit in my stomach hit rock bottom.

"I don't smell anything," Petey said softly.

"I don't *hear* anything," Bo whispered mockingly as his eyes widened, pretending to be afraid.

"Well, I take that back," said Petey. "I can smell Bo and dude, you stink. Did you do it again?"

"You're hilarious. Have I ever told you that?" Bo made a goofy face at Petey and turned back to me to make sure I saw it.

"Stop it, guys. I'm getting a funny feeling. Something isn't right," I said as I paced back and forth.

"Dude, you never, and I mean never come out with us. And *now* you're getting a funny feeling? I'm sorry, but I think we are a little more experienced than you in knowing what's up. And you know what's up?" Bo asked he shook his head. "Nothing. Okay? Nothing. Just chill."

"Yeah, it's okay," Petey agreed. "Let's just have some fun. A little hurt won't fun ya."

Bo grabbed Petey by the shoulders and shook him back and forth. "A little *fun* won't *hurt* ya. Get it right, son."

"That's what I said," Petey snarled as he brushed off Bo's grip. "It might even do you some good."

"Okay," I said as the fur on the back of my neck began to rise. I knew deep in my heart something was amiss but I didn't know exactly what.

"I'm going," Bo said as he took off again. "The kits are calling me."

I gazed above at the sky. The stars were beginning to come out. It was beautiful. The full moon had punched a hole in the nighttime, illuminating the sky. In the far distance I could hear the rushing sound of the Big River. Maybe the Big Woods *could* be interesting in the darkness.

A mighty group of fireflies buzzed past Petey and me, lighting up the night with a mysterious glow. Looking away, I noticed the most beautiful white flowers. I'd walked this way through the woods many times but had never seen them. In fact, I'd never seen anything like them. I stopped, letting Petey walk ahead.

"Last one over the Big River is a dirty little badger! Let's go!" Bo shouted, waving his arms wildly in the distance.

I dipped my nose to inhale the sweet smelling patch of huge white flowers.

"We're coming!" I heard Petey shout.

"Howard, what are you doing? Come on, let's go."

I ignored Petey as I stared in amazement at the beautiful tall flowers. "Petey, what are these?"

"I don't know. They're here every night. You'd know that if you came out with us more often. You just never stay out this late. Have you looked up?" Petey asked. "It's dark."

Petey put his hands on his hips and I could tell he was trying really hard to be a good friend. "Look, Howard, I'm glad you are with us tonight, but let's keep moving."

"Yeah, okay," I mumbled. "These flowers aren't here during the day."

"I wouldn't know. You're the only Nocturn that comes out during the day.

I'm catching my zzz's." Petey walked backwards as he spoke, egging me on.

"They smell great," I said, smiling and closing my eyes. I took a deep breath in, appreciating the aroma.

"Whatever. You're more of a flower guy than me," Petey replied. "Look, Bo is getting way ahead of us."

With that I could hear Bo shouting in the distance. "Hurry up, you little fur balls, I'm beating you both!"

"Come on, Howard," Petey begged. "Let's go. I don't want to listen to him razz us all night."

"I'm coming," I said, turning to take one final sniff of the fragrant white blooms. "Ahhh," I exhaled. "Flowers are one of the most wonderful gifts to the world. They are beautiful to the eye *and* the nose."

The moonlight danced off the white blooms and they looked like tiny angels opening their wings. "Do you think they open because of the moon?" I asked Petey.

I took a deep breath in and turned around. In an instant I knew – I was alone. And just when the night couldn't get any darker or worse – it did.

CHAPTER THREE
LOST

MY STOMACH CLENCHED in panic.
"Petey! Bo! Where are you?" I
shouted.

"Hurry, Howard! This way!" I could
hear them both in the distance and ran
frantically in circles on all fours trying to
calm myself. Where was I? How would I
get home?

Bo and Petey's voices faded like the
light in the sky as the clouds rolled in,
wrapping the heavens in a blanket. I
looked up at the darkness and wanted to

cry. The sky quickly turned black and the stars and the moon were gone.

I thought I could make out their distant laughter. I started running. I ran as hard and as fast as I could trying to catch up. When I thought I couldn't go any faster or farther I ran some more. My heart was pounding and my ears were ringing.

I stopped for a moment thinking I heard the sound of the Big River in the distance, but the only thing I heard was the boom-boom-boom in my chest that matched the throb in my head. Suddenly I felt sick. I was surrounded by tall, dry grass and knew logically I was far from water. I was in no way heading toward the Big River.

Everything looked so different when the sun wasn't shining. I couldn't tell where I was. I stood very still to listen to the night, hoping my friends' voices would call to me. Silence.

"No!" I cried as I walked through a pile of brush and limbs. "No!"

A huge light blinded me and I saw the word *Chevy*. In a *whoosh* of air and a loud *roar* I was knocked off my feet and showered with rocks. In a haze of smoke and pebbles I landed on my back – a ball of fur filled with fear.

I climbed back into the brush trying to catch my breath, and laid on my back in the dirt closing my eyes tightly. I wanted it to all go away but I needed to get home. Now I knew more than ever the darkness was no place for me.

"Chevy," I whispered into the night as my warm breath made a cloud in the cold air and I realized how my grandfather got his name.

I brushed myself off and quickly noticed a new smell. It was getting foggy. "No," I said aloud. "Smoke."

"Fire! Fire!" I shouted. But there was no one to hear me. I backed up quickly, stumbled over a rotten tree branch and fell to the ground flat on my back. Scrambling to my feet I found the remains of an old chewed up cigar, still smoldering.

"The evil of which we do not speak," I whispered.

The fire was getting higher and hotter, and my panic level rose. I covered my mouth and coughed uncontrollably. I needed to get to the river, and fast. I knew it was north in the Woods. Scurrying to the closest tree I quickly felt around its trunk.

Moss grows on the north side of the tree. If I could find the fuzzy green plant under my paws I could find my way. I slid to the ground and as soon as I felt the velvety smoothness, I looked above at the stars to get my bearings. There in the cloudy dark night the North Star broke through the inky sky just enough to guide me.

I burst through the tall grass with lightning speed. The fire was getting closer and I ran as fast as my legs would work. If the evil of which we do not speak was close it could mean real danger. I needed to warn Petey and Bo. If only I could find them.

Out of breath and away from the blaze, I looked over my shoulder, following a sound. I prayed it was my friends. I ran past the same beautiful flowers I'd admired earlier and relaxed a little, thinking I was going in the right direction.

As I got farther away I noticed the quiet stillness of the Big Woods. I could hear the crickets chirping and suddenly the dark night became blacker and emptier.

"Woof, woof, woof!"

Terrified, I stopped and froze in my tracks.

"Woof, woof, woof! Woof, woof, woof!" The barking overlapped this time and I knew there were two of them, maybe three.

I ran in a circle. I had to think, and think fast. Behind me, fire—in front of me, dogs. To my left, darkness. To my right, flashlights – flashlights and dogs. And these weren't just dogs. They were coonhounds. The evil of which we do not speak wasn't just out in the Big Woods; he was out in the Big Woods looking for *me*.

I dodged right and left, zigzagging as quickly as possible away from the fire and dogs. Suddenly the ground was wet and I knew I'd made it to a section of the river bottoms where it was muddy. I needed to cover my tracks. If I could make it to even a little bit of water the dogs would lose my scent.

Quietly I followed along the edge of the river, tracking through the mud. Splashing through the water and getting wet enough to cover my smell, I scampered up an enormous oak.

Grabbing the lowest branch of the massive tree, I made my way to the first, and then the next, and the next branch – my paws scratching against the old bark as I reached higher, stretching my body over and over. When I was high above the Big Woods, I crouched low in the shadow of a deep branch and trying to catch my breath.

"Woof, woof, woof! He's here somewhere. I can smell him!" snapped a hound.

"Me too!" barked the other. "We better keep looking. Master will have your hide!"

"My hide? What about yours? You're the one who lost him way back there!" They lumbered off out of breath, fighting amongst themselves.

I cowered in a ball of fur on the sturdy limb and held on for dear life. As the barking became more distant I opened one eye and one eye only, peeking out just enough to check if the flashlights were gone.

"You can breathe now," said a deep voice in the darkness.

Just when I thought the night couldn't get any darker or worse – it did.

CHAPTER FOUR
THE MESSENGER

COMPLETELY STARTLED BY the voice I jumped, lost my balance and nearly fell from the tree. Scrambling, I clung to the branch with my tiny paws. Struggling to the limb and managing to right myself, I once again curled up and began to shake so hard the surrounding leaves trembled as if they were as afraid as I was.

"Who are you?" I asked cautiously.

A pair of eyes opened and blinked in the dark night sky.

"Whooo?" asked the deep and gentle voice. "Whooo? My name is Waldron."

I knew Waldron. Of course I'd never met him, but I'd talked about him plenty. I'd made fun of Waldron in the past. I would ask other Nocturns why they would listen to the old owl and I wondered if Waldron knew this about me.

"My name is Howard," I stammered sheepishly.

"Howard," Waldron said with an air of authority. "I know whooo you are. It seems you are having an unfortunate evening."

"You could say that."

"Do you want to talk about it?"

"I'm not sure what you mean," I replied as I scooted back to where the limb met the trunk as if there was somewhere to hide.

"It looks as if you aren't going anywhere for a while," Waldron cooed as he looked over his shoulder at the flashlights in the distance.

The way Waldron twisted and turned his neck made it seem as though his eyes were floating in the night. It was unsettling and I wanted to tell him to keep his head screwed on straight. He was freaking me out.

"You certainly seem as if you need to catch your breath," Waldron continued. "Why don't you tell me about your adventure?"

A breeze blew in from the north and parted the clouds, and I could make out more than just Waldron's eyes. I could see his face. He had a huge beak and the eyebrows over his bright eyes made him look stern even though his voice was reassuring. He blinked with purpose and was constantly surveying the area below the big oak tree. He spoke deliberately and with such commanding power. I was in awe of him.

I had mixed emotions about spilling my guts to someone I'd been so openly critical of. I'd made it perfectly clear to everyone I didn't want to be a Nocturn. I'd also made no secret to others that I found it illogical to take advice from Waldron or Nicodemus. I didn't know if I wanted to open up to the great owl in the tree. But where else was I going to go?

"What was your plan tonight, Howard?" asked Waldron.

"I dunno. I don't go out at night."

"I see. So why were you out *tonight*? Off to visit my old friend Mr. Evron, perhaps?"

I swallowed the lump in my throat but didn't say a word. I tucked my head into my chest and rocked back and forth. I was terrified. I realized Waldron knew of my antics with Bo, playing tricks on the old blind bat.

"Or maybe you were just playing with some friends tonight. It is a beautiful evening– even if you are only out to smell the moon lilies."

"What did you say?"

"Moon lilies. The flowers. They only open at night," he said, unfurling his wings as if to demonstrate.

"I stopped to smell them. I'd never seen them before. That's when I lost Bo and Petey."

"Yes, I know," said Waldron, folding his wings and turning his head in a complete circle again.

"Can you *not* do that?" I asked as I hid my eyes. "You're freaking me out with the three-sixty-head-thing-a-ma-jig."

Waldron said nothing.

You saw?" I asked. "You saw what? Me smelling the flowers?"

Again Waldron remained silent.

"Why didn't you say something? Why didn't you help me find my friends? Can you help me find them now? Can you help me find my way home?"

"Why did you stop to see the flowers, Howard?" Waldron asked calmly.

"Why does it matter?"

"Everything matters, Howard."

"I stopped because I thought they looked like angels opening their wings. I've never seen them before," I said, suddenly defeated.

"Why have you never seen them?"

"I guess because they only bloom at night," I replied with a sniff, dropping my head into my paws. "And I won't come out at night."

Waldron turned his face away. "Why is that?"

After losing my friends in the dark, scrambling through flames and running from coonhounds – trying to educate the creepy owl on my logical-thinking-in-the-daylight-hours didn't seem like such a good idea. Especially when I knew he wanted to speak with me about the Keepers of the Night.

"I'm afraid of the dark," I confessed.

"I see," said Waldron, blinking his eyes tightly and eerily gliding his thick neck around, looking the opposite direction.

"What are we going to do about that?" Waldron asked very matter-of-factly.

"What do you mean?"

"Well, my boy, you are a Nocturn and by all accounts, a fine one at that."

Wiping my eyes with my paws and washing my hands, I looked up at Waldron without lifting my head and quietly asked, "How do you figure that?"

"It's my job to keep a watchful eye on things in the Big Woods. That means all the Nocturns." Waldron turned his head and looked at me. "I've been keeping an eye on *you*."

"Yeah?" I asked with an edge of sarcasm. "You've been watching *me*? I'll bet that's been pretty entertaining, huh?"

"Howard, you are an interesting case at that. But everyone is afraid of something. That is one of the lessons of life, my son. It is in the *facing of the fear* that you become."

"Become what, exactly?" I asked.

"You, Howard," Waldron explained as he turned up his wings. "Everyone has a purpose in the Big Woods. Do you know yours?"

"Is this where you tell me I'm supposed to be like my dad? I'm supposed to be a Keeper of the Night? *That's* never going to happen. I don't know who I am or what I want. I mean, how am I supposed to know?"

"Trust what you feel," said Waldron as he closed his eyes and pulled his wings in tightly.

"I trust what I *see*." I paced back and forth on the big oak limb.

"All that you see with your eyes will teach you to trust in all that you *do not* see with your eyes. Listen to your life, Howard, look with your heart. Your purpose is calling to you."

"What is that even supposed to mean?" I asked with exasperation. "Believe me, nothing is calling me – especially in the night."

"Have you ever seen a leaf fall from a tree, Howard?"

"Don't be silly." I stopped my pacing to look at Waldron. "Of course."

"Where does it land?"

"On the ground. The ground is the logical answer," I explained. "When something falls, the gravity of the earth pulls the object toward the center of the planet. Every object in the universe that has mass exerts a gravitational pull on every other mass."

"Not everything in life makes perfect sense, Howard."

"What do you mean?"

"When a leaf falls, it lands wherever the wind takes it."

"That's just air resistance," I explained proudly.

"That's fate. Howard, you, like all Nocturns, are a leaf. All you have to do is listen to the wind."

I turned away from Waldron and thought about what he said. I closed my eyes to listen intently to what the wind might want to tell me at that very moment.

"BAM! BAM! BAM!" Shots rang out from behind the tree and dogs barked wildly. Startled, I turned in a complete and tight circle on the tree limb.

"What should we do now, Waldron?" I asked in a whisper.

But he was gone. And just when the night couldn't get any darker or any worse, it did.

CHAPTER FIVE
A PURRRFECT PAIR

I KNEW THAT I had to get out of the tree before the dogs circled back and caught wind of my scent. I'd fooled them once, but I didn't know if I would be able to fool them again. In the distance I could see the flashlights. I'd wait for a moment, head north once again to the Big River and then go due east to get back home.

As soon as I saw the flashlights change direction I scurried down the oak tree and through the creek bed to kill my trail. I glanced up to the sky and ran as quickly as

I could, following the North Star to the Big River.

All I could think about was how Waldron had said I needed to listen to the wind and that he'd been watching me. Me? A Keeper of the Night? Who was he kidding? *I* was a darn fine Nocturn? What was that? I thought of myself as a lot of things, but never a Nocturn and certainly never a Keeper of the Night.

Stopping for a moment, I looked around and checked the sky to make sure I was still going north in the tall grass. With no flashlights in sight I could still smell the smoke but I couldn't see fire. I took two steps and caught a whiff of something yummy. Turning around I saw a house and gasped for air. "The evil of which we do not speak," I whispered.

Lights were on inside the house and I began to back up slowly. I had no idea how I'd stumbled into such danger, but I needed to stumble my way out again.

"For the love of catnip," purred the voice. "What the –? Oh…it's *you*."

"Who's there?"

"What does it matter anyway? You're going to run from the paw that feeds me."

"What?" I asked as I came closer to the voice attached to the purr.

It was Kit, the cat who lived with the evil of which we do not speak.

"Yes," she purred. "I lie about all day and they do whatever I bid them to do. I have full control over the paw that feeds me."

"It's a *hand*," I said, correcting her and her self-assured nature.

"Whatever. It does whatever I tell it to do."

"Why wouldn't you want to do for yourself? Why would you want to depend on anyone else —especially the evil of which we do not speak?"

"Because I can," she purred. "Why would you ever want to be alone and without someone to do it all for you? Here I am, my every need taken care of. And there you stand – all alone."

I looked at Kit lazing about in front of the house and watched the window to make sure no one was coming. "Standing alone doesn't mean I *am* alone. It means I'm strong enough to handle things by myself."

"Whatever," she purred as she licked her paw and gazed at me as if no one mattered except her.

The light inside the house shifted and I knew the evil of which we do not speak was inside. It suddenly occurred to me as I watched Kit lie on her back and paw at the night sky that the lazy cat could be of service to me.

"I want to make you a proposition, Kit. You know, I scratch your back, you scratch mine."

"I'm perrrrfectly fine right here, darling," she purred. "Why do I need you to scratch my back?"

"If you'll help me – give me information about the evil of which we do not speak, I can make sure the other Nocturns stay out of the trash," I said, thinking of Petey and his expert garbage grabbing. "You won't get blamed for it anymore."

I could see the wheels turning in that empty head of hers and knew I had her hooked. "What do I have to do – exactly?"

She sat up and her eyes glowed in the night, making her look like an evil monster when she was really just a lazy cat.

"You're one of the few that is up during the daytime like I am. If I come around and visit you – here, by the side of the barn and out of sight – you can tell me what you see inside the house."

"I see all sorts of things," she said as she lay back down again and looked away suddenly uninterested.

"Do this or I can guarantee the trash will be a mess every night. Do you want that?"

"No," she hissed. She stared at me as if she could read my mind. "What sort of things am I supposed to tell you?"

"Words like trap, gun, hunt – if you hear those you tell me. Is it a deal?"

"You leave me no choice," Kit purred as she turned and began to slink away.

A bright light suddenly glowed over the door of the barn and I knew I had to go. I had to go now. I heard the screen door slam from the back of the house and just when the night couldn't get any darker or worse – it did.

CHAPTER SIX
THE LOVELY LENA

I RAN FROM the backside of the barn and into the deepest part of the Big Woods without checking the night sky. I didn't even bother with where I was going. I knew I needed to stay away from the dogs, the fire and the evil of which we do not speak.

I ran as fast as I could and when the light over the barn was merely a speck in the night, I slowed down and caught my breath.

Sitting on the edge of an old mossy log, I tried to calm myself. I needed to think. It was then I noticed a mysterious glow circling overhead.

"Who's there?"

"Good evening, Howard," said the melodic voice.

Her glow was magical, and the light she cast caused me to squint my eyes. Her long eyelashes batted and I was at once mesmerized. She was intoxicating. Flapping her wings, the breeze she created was filled with what I could have sworn was the smell of cupcakes. It was wonderful.

Her name was Lena, and I thought she was the most magnificent luna moth in the entire world – let alone the Big Woods.

"Lena," I gasped. "You scared me."

"I'm sorry, my friend," she whispered in her tiny voice. "You look like you've seen a ghost."

"Lena, you can't imagine what I've seen tonight," I droned. "It's been one catastrophe after another. What are you doing out tonight?"

"I'm just flying east to meet up with some cousins. They are just recently out of the cocoon."

"East?" I immediately looked to the sky for the North Star. "You need to head this way," I said, pointing to the right.

"Really? How do you know?" she asked, batting her eyes wildly and making my heart race.

"That's the North Star. So if you are heading east, you need to go right."

I reached over to the nearest tree trunk to feel for moss. "And moss grows on the north side of the tree trunks," I laughed nervously. "Not all of them. Not this one. But that way is east."

I'd fallen all over myself and made not one bit of sense but that's what Lena did to me. My tongue got fat and my words didn't come out the way I wanted them to.

"Wow, Howard. Thank you."

Her words, on the other hand, melted into the air. "You seem to be in a hurry." Lena simultaneously batted her wings and lashes. "I won't keep you. It *is* lovely to see you tonight. I never get to see you in the evening, Howard —I mean, out with the Nocturns."

"Yeah, I know," I said, dropping my head in embarrassment. Looking up to the sky I gained a little strength. "But that's going to change. You'll be seeing a lot more of me."

"I'd really like that, Howard. We need you around here at night."

"Really?" I asked, feeling myself blush.

"You know a lot about the Big Woods. How did you learn all of that?" she asked.

I puffed up and tried to sound authoritative. "Observation, I guess. I like to know everything that's going on around me. I mean on the planet – or in the Big Woods." I was stumbling through my words and I knew I wasn't making much sense. I was saying words but thinking only of her. "I like to know how things work and why. Lena, your wings are so beautiful," I said quickly, changing the subject and making a fool of myself.

"Thank you, Howard," she sighed as she flapped them in the night air and flashed me a smile.

My stomach twisted with excitement. "Are they always this beautiful?" I asked as I swayed back and forth. "Or are they particularly amazing tonight?" I was desperately trying to be cool. It wasn't working.

"No," Lena said as the amazing smell of cupcakes wafted toward me. "You usually see me when the sun is beginning to set. My wings aren't as pretty in the daytime," she giggled. "They look best in the moonlight."

She fluttered her wings wildly and flew around my head several times, making me even dizzier.

"I'm just making the most of what I've got." She winked at me and suddenly I was without words.

"Hmm?" It was all I could manage to say.

"Well, I'm smaller than most of the other Nocturns and I'm more fragile. But I can do things other Nocturns cannot. So like I said, I'm just making the most of what I've got."

"And you've got a lot," I said with a goofy smile. "You're amazing. I'm just…me."

"It's easy to talk yourself out of being something amazing. So don't. All you have is you," she said, brushing my chest with her delicate arm. "Take care now, and don't be a stranger to the night."

"Oh, I won't!" I shouted after her. "You'll be seeing more of me!"

Away she flew and my mind was on everything *but* the night. "Ahhh…" I sighed. She was gone but I could still smell cupcakes. I stood alone in the Big Woods with a silly grin plastered across my face. "Make the most of me," I said aloud.

A strong wind picked up, and I thought maybe I knew exactly what Lena was talking about.

I felt a new sense of strength and took off running. I would be home soon, and well before the break of dawn. I puffed up my chest, ran a little faster and felt a little more confident. I'd survived half the night out in the darkness.

"Whoa!" I cried as I tripped and tumbled out of control in a ball of fur. I crashed into bushes, hit a rock and smashed into a tree. Just when I thought I'd finished crashing into everything in my path, I fell again. I flew through the air – rolling head over heels until I finally tumbled over a large hillside and hit my head on a mammoth sized rock at the bottom of a clearing. *Thud!* Just when the night couldn't get any worse or any darker, it did.

CHAPTER SEVEN
A Rock and a Hard Place

I WINCED AND tried to open my eyes. The image in front of me was blurry at first but I could smell something – rotten eggs or moldy garbage.

"Bo?" I called out, hoping my stinky friend was near.

I blinked harder, finally shutting my eyes tightly then opening them wide, hoping that would shake the fall from my dizzy head. When I focused, all I could see was teeth. All I could smell was bad breath.

"What tha—" I pushed myself onto my rear, trying to get away as fast as possible.

"If it isn't Howard The Coward," said the familiar raspy voice. "That fall looked like it hurt. Did it?"

Blinking harder, I rubbed my head and sat forward in a heap. I knew the voice. "Hi, Rock," I said as all the air in my lungs escaped.

Rock was the nastiest, meanest badger in the Big Woods. He was older than me and a lot bigger. His razor sharp teeth and silver grey hair seemed to stand on end at all times and I always thought Rock looked like a vampire. He was scary and his personality didn't help to dispel my fear.

Rock had fought everything you could think of in the Big Woods and won. He had the scars to prove it. He was one of the few Nocturns who'd fought the evil of which we do not speak and lived to tell the tale. He wasn't afraid of anything but I was afraid of him – and with good reason. He could break me in half if he wanted to and take anything he wanted. The problem was I didn't have anything to give him.

"So Howard the Coward." Rock circled me and spoke in a condescending tone. He'd always treated me like I was a baby – a baby who clearly didn't have a clue. "What in the wide, wide woods are you doing all the way out here? And so late at night?"

I couldn't shake the woozy feeling in my head. "Umm, I was out with Petey and Bo," I said, trying not to sound rattled. "They're just beyond the river." I hesitantly pointed in the direction I thought was north. Of course after the big tumble I was unsure which way was up.

"Oh yeah?" Rock asked. "Over there?" Rock pointed in the same direction as I did. "That's interesting."

"Y-Yeah?" I asked with a stutter, afraid my uncertainty was starting to show. "Why?"

"It's just that I saw both of them earlier tonight, and they said that you were…ah…lost," Rock said with a sarcastic smile as he circled me again, making me skittish.

I nervously began to wring my paws and swayed back and forth looking for any place to hide. The moonlight shone on the thorny brush behind the hole in the ground Rock called home and something glistened in the night and caught my eye.

"Do you need help?" Rock asked in a baby voice. "Does *wittle* Howard the Coward need help?"

"I'm not lost," I said, laughing it off as best I could as I moved closer to the glare in the brush. I leaned back as if I was stretching my body after the fall and spied a trap – a wire cage set out in the night by the evil of which we do not speak to catch Nocturns.

I needed to get out of Rock's lair and away from the trap. I looked around for anything that could show me which way was north while I played it as cool as I was capable. "I'm fine. Those guys – I mean, I was just playing with them. It's – it's cool," I stammered. "I'll just be leaving now."

"Really?" asked Rock. "Which way ya heading? Cause you know who's out tonight? I heard they already bagged a couple of coons. Anybody *you* know?"

"I'm sure everyone *I* know is safe. And thank you for your concern, but I know my way and I'll just be going now."

As I took a step toward the clearing to check the stars, I tripped over a root in the ground and fell on my head once again.

"Dog biscuits!" I sat in a heap, rubbed the huge knot on my head and looked down to my arm only to find a new gash. I rose from the ground quickly as Rock hurried alongside me.

"Whoa!" Suddenly I was on my back yet again looking up at the stars. Rock had tripped me.

"I don't have a clue what you are doing." Rock laughed and I immediately wondered if I could get him close to the trap. "Howard the Coward, you amuse me so."

I looked up to find him standing over me –my view of the stars now obstructed by his big head and sharp teeth.

"Watch your step there, buddy." He held his paw and razor-sharp nails out to me as if he wanted to help me up. I refused, got to my feet and inched closer to the trap.

"My friend," Rock said as he placed his arm around me. "Listen to me. I'll get you out of here and on your way."

In that moment, I noticed a fresh bloody scar on his leg from a recent fight. I knew what I had to do.

Quickly turning into his body, I spun out of his grip and gave him a quick push right into the path of the set trap. With two stumbling steps backward, Rock fell into the cage and the door immediately snapped shut.

"Look what you've done, you stupid little raccoon. I'm gonna kill you!" Rock shouted.

I circled the trap once to get a better look, staying as far away from Rock's claws as I could. Over and over he grabbed at me from behind the woven mesh trap.

"Get me out of here. NOW!" Rock flew into a fit of rage and rattled each side of the trap as he jerked and threw his body around inside the cage. Quietly I watched, not saying anything. I knew I needed to use this situation to my best advantage.

"You've got to help me!" he shouted.

"I don't have to do anything," I replied as I kept my distance and watched him twist his body, slamming it against the sides of the metal causing a clang.

His chest heaved in and out as he gasped for breath. "What do you want?" he panted.

I thought for a moment. What *did* I want from Rock? I knew from looking at the cage I could release him, but what did I want in return?

"Tell me something, Rock." I circled the trap and watched as Rock matched each move I made with his own. "You aren't afraid of anything. Are you?"

"No!" he shouted as his body jumped again, rattling the cage in anger.

I stepped away from him and watched his wrath unfold. "Everyone's afraid of something –Waldron said so. And yet you are afraid of nothing. Why?"

Rock stared at me and huffed. "Why should I tell a little pipsqueak like you how to be brave? You're afraid of the dark!"

I nodded and began to walk away. "See you around, Rock."

"Wait!" he shouted over my shoulder. "Can you get me out of here?"

I stopped in my tracks but didn't turn. "Yes."

"Come back."

I turned and walked back to see Rock standing at the front of the cage, calmer than before. He gripped each side of the trap with his long claws and looked right in my face.

"The fear. It needs you."

"What?" I asked.

"The fear needs you to survive. *You* fuel the fear—not the outside world, and certainly not the Big Woods."

"I fuel the fear?"

"Everyone does. Not me, but…" he hesitated. "Yeah. That's it."

"I'm a smart guy, Rock, and what you're saying doesn't make any sense."

"Well, it does, and you're not that smart if you don't understand it." Rock gave me a heavy sigh. "And you're not going to help me out of here until you do understand, so let me say it again. The fear is what you should be afraid of and nothing else. Only *you* can fuel fear and only *you* can take its power away."

I thought about what he was saying to me. "I give my fears their power over me?"

"Now you're starting to get it," Rock said sarcastically. "See, I'm awesome. I know I'm awesome. And I'm awesome because you and nobody else is ever going to convince me otherwise."

I looked at him and tried to digest all that he was saying. "You're awesome because you say you're awesome?"

"You become what you believe you are. If you believe you're afraid of the dark then you'll be afraid of the dark. If you think you're smart then you'll be smart. I know I'm awesome and I am...*awesome*."

He looked at me as if he'd just dispensed life-changing advice. And perhaps he had.

"I fuel the fear," I repeated.

"Yeah. Now get me outta here."

"Step back," I said as I pulled the catch lever at the top of the cage and held it while Rock hurried out of the trap. It closed again with a snap and he was free.

"Thanks," Rock huffed.

"Don't mention it," I replied.

"Don't worry. I won't."

Ignoring Rock but thinking about what he said, I walked to the bottom of the cliff and looked up from where I came. "Hmmm…" I sighed.

"That's the long way. There's a shortcut."

"What?"

"There's a shortcut. Go around this hill and then up."

I let out a tiny gasp as Rock narrowed his gaze. I could see my own reflection in his eyes. It was an odd moment for me. I was in the lair of the scariest beast in the

Big Woods and yet I wasn't letting my fear of him rule me.

Rock smacked me hard on the back as if we were friends, knocking the wind out of me. "Take my word for it," he said. "Go around. Then you can get back with your other little stupid friends and do whatever it is that you do at night."

I paused for a moment. A shortcut did sound better. I looked down at my bloody paws and felt the lump on my head. For once, I wanted something to be easy.

"You wouldn't jerk me around, would you?" I asked.

"That's not my style, bro." Rock gave me a crooked smile and I didn't know if I could trust him or not, but I decided to give him a shot.

"Okay." I walked away without saying goodbye or looking back. I didn't want to. I didn't need to.

I picked up speed as I traveled the path. If this was a shortcut I wanted to make the best of it. The longer I walked the more I realized I was going in circles.

"I should've known better. Rock just wanted me to be even more lost," I said aloud and with a sigh. And just when the night couldn't get any worse or any darker, it did.

CHAPTER EIGHT
SLIPPERY STUFF

I'D BEEN RUNNING in circles for a good while and although I wasn't afraid, my arm ached where I'd fallen and my head still pounded from ramming into the tree.

I spotted a patch of marigolds and stopped to pick a few and carefully chewed them. Taking the mashed flowers out of my mouth, I spread the sticky goo onto my bleeding arm. The marigolds had healing properties and I knew this because I'd read it in a book Petey found for me. As I soothed my throbbing arm, I realized

I was going to have to backtrack. I'd wasted too much time as it was. I was mad at Rock for putting me on the wrong path, but I wasn't surprised. It was my own fault for listening to him and not listening to my own common sense.

I finally made it back to my original route and I stopped for a moment to breathe. I was weary and I really had no idea how long I'd been out. From the look of the stars in the sky, dawn would be breaking soon and I thought about the conversation my grandfather had with Violet and me earlier in the night.

Every day just before the sun goes down and the moon comes out, there is a perfect moment in time —Twilight. "I need to find my purpose."

My paws were bloody from the fall down the hill, my head scraped and my pride worn. I'd been through fire, chased by dogs, lectured by an owl, badgered by, well…a badger. What *was* my purpose?

I spied Rock's lair in the distance and began to climb the hill that had been so unkind to me earlier. With a deep breath I got a strong foothold and began to scale the steep hillside. Little by little, inch by inch, I made my way up the rock wall. Carefully I switched from rock to limb, to tree root, back to rock, to overhang. I didn't let go of one paw until the other was secure.

I gripped a large, exposed root of a tree hanging off the side of the hill and just as I was reaching for the next spot to grasp, I heard it.

"Sssaaay…" The snake slithered onto the tree branch and over my head. I was looking eye to eye with Jake the snake. Startled, I began pedaling my legs, trying to catch hold of anything stable.

"Jake! You scared me! Sheesh!" I let out a sigh, having found a foothold on a rock below. Jake was a two-foot garter snake. He always seemed to show up at inopportune moments. If I was having a horrible day, Jake was always there to document it.

"What are you doing out tonight, Howard?" Jake hissed. "You don't come out at night."

"Well, I —"

"It'sss way passst your bedtime, bud-dy," Jake said, cutting me off. "And sssooo far away from your home, too."

"Yeah, well —"

"And you are ssstuck on this gnarly hill? How are you ever going to get home? And in the dark? You hate, and I mean *hate*, the dark. Am I right?"

Jake continued to slither back and forth, writhing around the tree branch. I decided to ignore him and keep moving onward and upward, but Jake wouldn't be quiet.

"Really, Howard, I am curiousss. How did you get here?" Jake asked, his eyes widening. Jake had a slimy way about him. Whenever my mother was around Jake was always overly nice to her. He was mean when no one was looking, but a model Nocturn when adults were around. It was dishonest and creeped me out.

"I guess I just sort of fell onto this path." I let out a little laugh, trying to sound nonchalant.

Jake slithered around my arm, down my leg, and back up again as I screamed,

"Yikes! Knock that off! What the heck are you doing?"

"You've got quite a few bumpsss and bruisesss, Howard," hissed Jake. "How are you ever going to make it home like that?"

"I'll be just fine, thank you. Now please stop slithering all over my arm."

"What will you give me if I do?" Jake hissed.

"What?" I was trying desperately to get a better foothold on the side of the hill, but each time Jake wriggled around me it tickled and I thought I might plummet back into the clearing.

"Why do I have to give you something?"

"Becaussse I need more."

"More *what*?" I asked as I adjusted my grip.

"Ssstuff. One can never have enough thingsss. They make me happy."

"You have things but no friends, Jake," I said, not thinking my words through before saying them.

I watched the wheels in Jake's tiny brain turn and I knew he was either going to understand me and let me pass, or make sure I ended up in a pile at the bottom of the cliff.

"I don't need friendsss. I like my thingsss."

"That's fine," I said. "But you can't run around the Big Woods dragging all the things you've taken from other Nocturns. You can laugh and play with friends – but you don't have any. Now, I'm not giving you anything to pass and if you don't get off of my arm, I'll throw you to the bottom of this hill myself. Got it?"

I began to climb again, finding strength from deep within. I'd just taken another step on the outside of the treacherous hillside when Jake laughed and said, "Persssonally, I don't think you have a leaf'sss chance in a ssstrong wind of making it home tonight."

"What did you say?" I asked as I knitted my brow and glared down at him.

"I said, persssonally I don't think you have…"

"A leaf's chance in a strong wind of making it home tonight," I said, finishing his sentence. I looked at him blankly. "That's what I *thought* you said. Excuse me—I've got things to do."

I continued to climb without looking back. And just when I thought things couldn't get any better, they did.

CHAPTER NINE
THE VOICE OF REASON

WITH A HARRUMPH I struggled to make it to the top of the hill. The question was which hill was I on top of?

"Where in the Sam Hill am I?" I giggled out loud, thinking of Bo and Petey. If they could only see me now – beaten up and bruised – lost. I laughed out loud again and looked up to the sky – clouds, no North Star to guide me, and not a tree in sight. I decided I'd just have to make it on my instincts.

The longer I walked the more I realized I wasn't getting any closer to home. I was, in fact, going farther and farther away from the Big Woods and the river. I knew this because the land was getting hillier and drier, and my stump was in the river bottoms. I had no choice but to wait until the sky cleared and get on the right path.

I found the edge of a wooded area and sat down for a moment to rest on an old rotten log. I gazed up at the sky and watched the clouds as they began to lift. I could tell by the shift in the heavens and the change in the color of the sky that dawn would be breaking soon. A strong wind blew from the east, ruffling my fur and sending a shiver up my back. The leaves flew past me, reminding me of what Waldron said.

"Listen to the wind, Howard." The voice was low but clear. Where was it coming from? I stood and turned around in circles, looking everywhere. Then I heard it again.

"Listen to the wind." The voice was deep and comforting.

"Who...who's there?" I stammered. I wasn't afraid, but I was curious.

"Dawn will be breaking soon. Let the Twilight guide you."

"Who are you? Where are you?" I asked in bewilderment.

"I'm your friend, Nicodemus."

I was astonished, scared, excited, and relieved all at the same time. "Where are you? *What* are you?" I whispered as I frantically searched everything around me. Looking up in the trees and through the woods I found nothing and no one. I was so excited I couldn't catch my breath, and at that very moment I saw him. His huge antlers cast a moonlit shadow across the clearing where I stood. He must have had seventy points on his rack. Nicodemus was old – very old.

"Howard, why are you running?"

"How do you know my name?"

The massive deer said nothing as I watched his nostrils fill the cold night air with warm breath. I knew he wasn't going to tell me. I decided to just answer his question. "I'm not running. I've been chased all night."

"You've been running long before tonight. You've been running from yourself since you were just a kit."

His voice was like a whisper, but no whisper I'd ever heard before.

"I like the daytime. And... well—" I hesitated, kicking the dirt at my feet and looking at the scrapes on my paws. "To be honest, I'm just not very good at being a Nocturn."

"You are *very* good at being exactly who you are, Howard. Tonight, when you became lost, what did you do first?"

"I panicked," I explained. "I ran in circles for so long, I lost my head. And then…and then…" I continued, "I lost my friends."

"Yes," said Nicodemus calmly. "Go on. What did you learn?"

"That I shouldn't go out at night?" I asked, half joking.

"No, Howard. What did you do?"

"I checked the sky for the North Star and the moss on the trees," I said as if it was no big deal.

"Why?"

"Because I knew that the Big River was north."

"But how did you know the stars in the sky?"

"I studied them, of course," I explained, as if everyone did such things.

"And how did you know that moss grows on the north side of a tree?"

"Because of the way the sun shines on the earth."

"Do you think that other Nocturns know these things?" asked Nicodemus.

"I never really thought that much about it. I don't see much of the other Nocturns," I said, stepping closer to get a better look. All I could really make out was his shadow and his enormous set of antlers.

Nicodemus snorted and took a step back. "Why did you cross through the river when the evil of which we do not speak came near?"

"So the dogs would lose my scent. They lose my trail if I can cut through even a little bit of water."

"How did you know that?"

"I just knew."

"You made a deal with Kit the cat tonight."

"But…" I stammered, moving in closer. "How did you know that?"

Nicodemus said nothing but merely waited on me to continue. "I made the deal so she would tell me about the evil of which we do not speak."

"Why?"

"To protect my friends and family."

"Why did you stop and put the marigolds on your cut?"

"To make it feel better, I suppose. Marigolds have healing properties. There are other plants that have them too, but marigolds were what I found first," I said, wondering why Nicodemus was asking so many questions.

"But how did you know to use them, Howard?"

"I just knew," I said as I watched Nicodemus' huge antlers nod in approval.

"Howard, you're not only a Nocturn, you're special. You are a Keeper of the Night."

"But I'm not! I'm afraid!" I cried, throwing my face into my paws. I was suddenly again very unsure of myself.

"And so too are most of the Nocturns in the night, as are most of the daytime animals. Every creature has fears. It is in the fabric of our being. Fear, joy, love, sadness—they all exist together. It is how you interact within them that matters the most, Howard."

"Rock told me not to fuel my fear."

"This is good advice, but Rock cannot control his anger and if you fear nothing, you become complacent – vulnerable. You don't have to be afraid, but you do need to be cautious."

I listened intently as the moon had once again come alive in the night sky. I looked up to the heavens and noticed that the moon seemed to be shining brightly on my fur as if something magical was about to happen.

"It is not only with your eyes that you see, not only with your ears that you hear, not only with your paws that you touch – but with your heart and soul that you look, listen, feel, and learn much from this world and each other," continued Nicodemus. His words moved in harmony with the moonlight. "Nocturns are special, Howard. We have the ability, more so than any other creatures on earth, to know this because we live in the darkness. In the night you must look with your heart, and not just your eyes."

"It's just so…dark. Aren't you ever afraid?"

"In the day the stars are always in the heavens but when the sun is shining it's too bright to see them. Stars cannot shine without the darkness, Howard. Some things, like stars, are most beautiful and most useful when times are dark."

Nicodemus was somehow making sense to me. I put my paws on my hips and closed my eyes, trying my best to process the logic of the illogical. "I'm not my dad, you know. I kinda feel like you're telling me all of this as if I was just a smaller version of my father. I'm not. He was a hero. I'm Howard the Coward."

"Your father was a very brave Keeper of the Night, and you *are* like your father. But if you continue to tell yourself you're a coward, a coward is what you'll be. What *you* think of yourself is much more important than what others think of you. I urge you to look beyond what you see before you – what you think others expect you to be. Open your heart, Howard. There is a whole new world for you if you do."

I looked into the woods where Nicodemus stood. The moon had shifted in the night sky. Dawn was beginning to break.

"Nicodemus? What happens at Twilight?"

"What do you want to happen?"

"My grandfather says you can find purpose. But what is my purpose?"

"Just as the sun knows to rise and set, and the moon knows to cast its all-knowing light on us, you too will know. Remember, Howard, it's not always in the being, it's in the knowing."

"But I don't know that I can *really* –you know–*believe* what you are saying to me," I said. "I want to. I'm trying to."

"Howard," Nicodemus said as he stepped closer to the moonlight, "I've been around for eons. I could tell you that I've seen it all. But what I'll say instead is that everything I've come to understand in this world has taught me that I should have faith for all that I *don't* understand."

"Wait!" I shouted, putting my paw up abruptly. "Are you saying to believe in what I can't see or hear? No matter what?"

"Faith," Nicodemus said. "When you look with your heart you will see what is invisible to the eye."

"Invisible to the eye," I repeated, pacing back and forth, trying to understand. "And my purpose – how do I know when I've found my purpose?"

"Every creature on earth is born with a map – a map that's hidden in your soul. That map will lead you."

"So how do I find it?" I asked, still not following.

"Only one way, my son," he said. "Your compass. Your heart."

I put my hand to my chest and rubbed my own heart, wanting to make sense of it all.

"And here's the magic, Howard," continued Nicodemus. "The heart whispers only to the soul. Listen closely and you'll always stay on course."

"I don't know that I have a compass."

"Everyone has a compass. You have one of the best compasses ever made, Howard. The question isn't if you have one. The question is, are you following it?"

I didn't answer. I stared at him for a long moment before dropping my head. "Will I see you again?"

"That depends," Nicodemus said as he turned his back to walk away.

"My granddad says I'm nothing less than myself."

"Nothing less than yourself, or maybe – just maybe – more than you ever thought you could be."

I looked into the deep of the Big Woods and just as quietly as Nicodemus had appeared, he was gone. I looked to the heavens and gave a huge sigh. It was nearly daybreak and just when I thought I'd never see daylight again, I found I could easily make my way back home.

CHAPTER TEN
A NEW DAY

I TOOK A few slow and deliberate steps out into the clearing and looked upward to the heavens. In the distance to the east, I could see the dark blue giving way to the orange and pink of the dawn. As the new colors pushed their way into the sky, I thought maybe God was painting a new picture for the day, as I suppose He did every day. I'd just never been around for the moment before.

While the colors of the beautiful twilight illuminated the sky, I took my grandfather's advice, stood up and opened my arms wide to the world. I closed my eyes and let the slowly rising sun shine on my upturned face. I could hear the sound of my heart beating wildly in my chest and I was beginning to realize how tired I was. It was time for bed. I could sleep all day, and I had *never* been able to sleep all day.

I took a huge breath. Anything was possible. *Everything I did today is in the past and tomorrow I can start anew.*

I made a vow to myself standing alone in the clearing – each night I would ask the Twilight for its blessings and guidance – and for the ability to look with my heart, as each new night in my life as a Nocturn unfolded.

I started down the path I absolutely knew led to my stump. My legs ached and my head hurt, but I didn't care. I ran as fast as I could. I was going home.

I felt a strong wind at my back. It ruffled my fur and blew dust all around me. I looked up to find Waldron swooping past me, flying overhead and mightily landing on the tree branch in the lane I was following.

"Waldron!" I yelled excitedly. "What are you doing here?"

"Good morning, Howard," Waldron said with authority. "I have a message for you."

"A message for me?" I asked as I stopped to catch my breath.

"Yes," replied Waldron. "Nicodemus would like for you act as a Keeper of the Night and explain to others of your adventure last night – including the evil of which we do not speak."

"I'm supposed to go back and hold a meeting with the Nocturns to teach them?" I asked with confusion. "That's what *you* do, Waldron."

"Yes, Howard, I'm well aware of my duties. Nicodemus is requesting *you*. Are you up to the task?"

"Sure. I mean, I guess," I said with hesitation. "I mean, yes! Tell Ole Nick I said, yes!"

I jumped in my tracks and turned around in a circle in excitement.

"I'll tell '*Ole Nick,*'" Waldron said sarcastically, "he can count on you."

Waldron stretched his massive wings and flew away, creating a burst of wind with each mighty flap and I caught a glimpse of what I could only believe to be a smile.

I picked up my pace as I traveled down the path that led through the Big Woods. "Me, teaching the other Nocturns. Wow!" I shouted as I continued to pick up speed.

A strong gust of wind blew and the leaves from a nearby tree took flight. I stopped and turned in a circle to watch them swirl in the breeze. A single leaf fell from the sky and onto my shoulder. I picked it up and studied it carefully. "Where are you taking me?" I asked in a whisper.

I laughed out loud, giddy with excitement and beat my chest dead center with my fist three times and held it to the sky. Suddenly I felt like I could conquer the world.

If the Nocturns were going to listen and trust in my words then I needed to listen and trust in my own heart.

I turned the corner of the woods and ran through a creek bed, past the tall grass and through the garden of white flowers that were now closed for the day. As I made it to the top of the hill, I stopped and looked down on the valley I called home. There it was – home sweet stump.

Meandering around the flower garden, I could see my family. "Hey!" I shouted, waving my arms wildly. "Hey! I'm up here!" They didn't hear me. I turned to look behind me one last time, not wanting to forget the night I'd just survived. I took a deep breath, feeling thankful. I was thankful for my family and friends, thankful for the Twilight of the morning, and thankful that I was a Nocturn.

I turned and faced my new life and began to calmly make my way home.

"What's all this?" I whispered aloud. I couldn't believe what I was seeing with my own eyes. There they were – all of them. Every Nocturn I'd ever known or seen. They were all standing together, waiting. But for what?

"How-ward!" shouted Violet as she pointed to me, drawing the other Nocturns' attention.

"Hey!" I shouted.

A huge roar erupted from the crowd and I was completely caught off guard. I lumbered down the hill as fast as I could as the crowd jumped and cheered. They were cheering for *me*.

Out from behind the stump I saw Petey and Bo. "Howard! My man!" shouted Bo. "Where in the wide, wide woods have you been? You missed a heck of a night!" he bragged as he gave me a pat on the back.

"No, *you* missed a heck of a night!" I yelled over the crowd, pointing to him.

"Yeah, yeah, yeah, I know. I heard," he said with a sly smile.

"Woo hoo!" yelled Petey, running to my side. "We looked everywhere for you!"

"I'm so glad to see you!" I shouted as I embraced Mom and Gran, pushing through my friends to get to them. My mother wet her paw and smoothed my ruffled fur.

"What is all this?" I asked, pointing to the crowd who continued to cheer and applaud my homecoming.

"Waldron has been here," gushed Gran with a gigantic smile. "He's told us some heroic tales of you, son. We're *so* proud. The newest Keeper of the Night."

"Were you woods in the lost?" asked Petey, rubbing me on the head and messing up my fur again.

"You could say that," I laughed, not wanting to correct him. Instead I put my arm around my friend to answer his question personally. "I was lost for a while but I finally found exactly what I was looking for."

Petey winked at me, turned to Bo, and shrugged his shoulders. "I have no idea what he's talking about."

Bo rolled his eyes and quietly said to Petey, "I'll explain it to you later."

"Waldron says you are holding a meeting," said Gran, pulling my attention away from my friends.

"Yes," I said as I walked to the stump, climbed up and stood tall. The crowd quieted down in order to hear what I was about to say.

"Hello, everyone. I'm Howard, and I'm a Nocturn." A thunderous round of applause came up from the group. I put my hands up to quiet the crowd. "Nicodemus has asked me to talk with you this morning about a few items…"

I spoke clearly and directly. I interjected humor while telling of my night in the woods. As I told my tale I put my paw over my heart, carefully following the new direction of my internal compass. If I listened to the world I might believe all the bad. But I would from this day forward listen with my heart. And I would only see the goodness around me. I was thankful for my night of struggles. Without it I never would have known how strong I could be.

In the night there isn't only darkness. In the night there is beauty, love and the chance to look with your heart. After all, a star shines brightest in the darkest of nights.

The End

To download The Nocturns Song
"Look with Your Heart" visit:
www.thenocturns.com

About the Author

K.C. Pottorf is a former copywriter and PR mercenary who began writing after her best friend talked her into it. *The Nocturns* is a story she wrote twenty years ago for her children who are now all grown up. She loves alliteration, pearls and post-it notes. She's married to the man of her dreams who makes music all day long and lives in Lexington, Kentucky. She's Momma to two kids, now in college – one at the University of Kentucky, and one at New York University-Tisch. She is also responsible for one very needy dog. K.C. also writes books for big people under the name Kris Calvert. When she's not writing, she's baking cupcakes.

About the Illustrator

Craig McKay was born a Buckeye, raised a Hoosier and now resides in the Peach tree State with his lovely wife and an ever-growing assortment of kitties and wiener dogs. Doodling since diapers, Craig has won numerous awards for his illustrations, including 3 prestigious division Honors from the National Cartoonists Society. When not coloring with his crayons, he is cheering for the Reds, watching cars go 'round in circles or working in his own personal Victory Garden. A further peek into his work can be found at: www.monkeywithcrayon.com.

WEBSITE

www.thenocturns.com

EMAIL

info@thenocturns.com

LOOK FOR US ON FACEBOOK

Made in the USA
Charleston, SC
08 December 2014